Disney · PIXAR

UP

THE INSIDER'S GUIDE

Disney · PIXAR

UP

THE INSIDER'S GUIDE

Written by
Laura Gilbert and
Julia March

CONTENTS

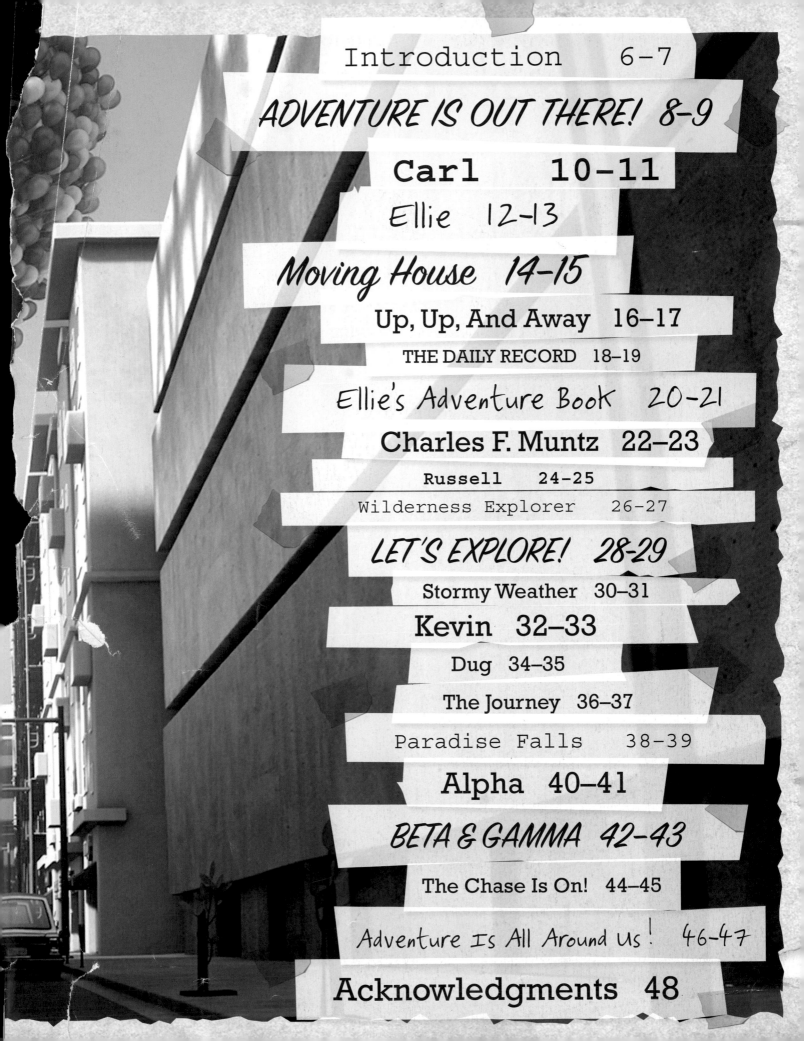

INTRODUCTION

For Carl Fredricksen, life is all about routine.
He wakes up to the sound of his alarm. He eats cereal at
his breakfast table. He vacuums his house from top to
bottom. Before he knows it, it's 3:30 p.m.—dinner time!
Carl thinks life will always be like this and he likes it
that way. But that's before a Junior Wilderness Explorer
comes knocking and his whole life is turned upside
down. Carl will learn that sometimes all you have to do
in order to change your life is to open your front door...

ADVENTURE IS OUT THERE!

Young Carl and Ellie are opposites: Carl is shy and stumbles over his words while Ellie is a talkative, confident tomboy. But they do have one important thing in common—they both love adventure! Ellie's wish is to go to Paradise Falls and the pair make it their lifelong goal to get there.

Brave Boy

Carl has to try a bit harder than Ellie to be adventurous. When he loses his balloon in Ellie's clubhouse, his attempt to reach it ends in a broken arm!

GRAPE SODA

Ellie gives Carl a badge made out of a grape soda bottle cap. Now they're adventurers together!

Sweet Dreams

Ellie shows Carl her Adventure Book filled with all the things she wants to do. Besotted Carl just hopes she will take him on all of her adventures.

In Carl's imagination, his blue balloon is an airship. He calls it the *Spirit of Adventure*, named after the dirigible of famous explorer Charles F. Muntz.

"You and me. We're in a club now!"

Ace Adventurer

Carl and Ellie's hero is the famous adventurer Charles F. Muntz. Muntz discovers exciting new lands and Carl and Ellie hope to one day do the same.

Falls Fund

Newlyweds Carl and Ellie know that dreams alone will not get them to Paradise Falls. They start saving money in a jar until they have enough to take the trip.

Carl and Ellie's time together flies by quickly. Before they know it they have grown old, and they still haven't made it to Paradise Falls.

Carl switches off his hearing aid when he doesn't want to listen to people around him.

CARL

Carl Fredricksen lives alone and he likes it that way. Carl wasn't always a grouch, though. When his wife, Ellie, was alive, the pair dreamed of adventure. Carl thinks those days are long gone but the arrival of a Junior Wilderness Explorer named Russell changes it all...

3 1833 05763 3270

Carl and Ellie met when they were youngsters. Every day was fun when the two of them were together.

Time Flies

In Carl's old age, he moves a lot slower and can't hear as clearly as he used to. His memory is still perfect though: he has not forgotten his promise to Ellie to go to Paradise Falls.

Ellie gave Carl this badge that she made out of a grape soda bottle cap.

Tennis balls on the end of Carl's cane help him to move about a bit quicker and they are handy when trying to lure animals away!

A construction company wants to demolish all the houses on Carl's block to make way for high-rise buildings. Carl's is the only house still standing.

Home Sweet Home

The house Carl lives in was originally Ellie's childhood clubhouse. On the mantel, Carl keeps Ellie's treasures, like her binoculars, photos, and tropical-bird figurine.

"What do I do now, Ellie?"

Carl used to sell balloons from a cart at the local zoo where Ellie worked.

Carl's mailbox is precious to him. It is decorated with Ellie and Carl's handprints and he won't give it up without a fight.

Did you know?

• Carl loves routine. Every day he eats the same breakfast, then vacuums every surface in the house.

When Russell offers to assist Carl, Carl tells him he does not want to be assisted. To get rid of Russell, Carl sends him off to find an imaginary bird called a snipe.

New Best Friend

Young Ellie is excited to have a new friend to play with. She can't wait to make Carl a member of her secret explorer's club.

"Thanks for the adventure— now go have a new one."

Ellie and Carl loved to take photos of every important moment in their lives together.

Perfect Couple

When young Ellie finds Carl in her clubhouse admiring her collection of Muntz memorabilia, she thinks they could become friends. She never imagined that they would one day marry and live in her old clubhouse!

ELLIE

Ellie saw adventure in everything! This lively tomboy loved playing in her clubhouse and sticking pictures in her Adventure Book. Her imagination took her on great adventures, though what she dreamed of most was to go to Paradise Falls like her hero Charles F. Muntz.

When a tree damages Carl and Ellie's roof, they have no option but to use money from their Paradise Falls fund to pay for repairs. It looks like their dream of flying to the falls is slipping away.

Ellie always put on Carl's ties for him. He never got the hang of it himself.

Happy Memories

Ellie may no longer be in Carl's life but he still has all his wonderful memories of her. Every day he kisses her photo and promises he will never forget her and the life they had together.

EXPLORER IN THE WILD

Ellie kept a scrapbook where she put all of her ideas for adventure.

Did you know?

• Ellie worked in the South America house at the local zoo. Her favorite animals were the colorful tropical birds.

MOVING HOUSE

Carl's house is the only one left standing on his block. A construction company wants to demolish all of the houses to make way for skyscrapers. Carl, however, has no intention of giving up his home. His house and belongings are all that he has left to remind him of Ellie. If the construction company thinks he's going to take this lying down, they can think again!

Hands Off

When a truck hits Carl's mailbox, construction worker Steve tries to fix it. Instead, he is hit in the head by Carl's walking cane!

Carl has never even hurt a fly before. He just doesn't want to lose his home. Carl is scared: what has he done?

Serious Business

The construction company means business. Suited and booted, the boss has made several offers of big money for Carl's house. All Carl has given him in exchange is prune juice in his gas tank!

14

Hard hats are good protection against walking canes.

Trying Time

Carl is summoned to court for hitting the construction worker. As he waits to be called into the courtroom, Carl is pretty sure this isn't the adventure Ellie wanted him to have.

After his court hearing, a policewoman drops Carl back at home. Carl won't be going to jail but he will be going to Shady Oaks Retirement Village... or will he?

The smiling couple on the front of the Shady Oaks brochure still doesn't sell Carl on the idea of leaving his home.

Long Goodbye

The Shady Oaks nurses come to take Carl to his new home. Carl asks for a minute to say farewell to his house. The truth is, he may need a bit longer...

15

UP, UP, AND AWAY

The nurses from Shady Oaks think Carl is going to say goodbye to his house but he's actually going to say goodbye to them! Within seconds, thousands of balloons emerge from Carl's chimney and the house ascends into the sky. The ultimate lift off!

Inspiration

Ellie used to pretend her clubhouse was an airship with ropes attached to a weather vane and a bicycle tire frame for a steering wheel. She sure gave Carl a few ideas!

On Their Way

Carl is determined to keep his promise to Ellie to take their house to Paradise Falls. If only she was here for the adventure.

16

Sails

Every flying house needs sails to help it soar. Carl uses whatever he can find to create sails: curtains, clothes, and quilts attached to curtain rods.

Balloons

Balloon strings hang down into Carl's fireplace. When Carl wants to sail the house lower, he cuts a few strings.

Steering

A complicated system of ropes, pulleys, and a steering handle allows Carl to guide his house through the sky.

17

THE DAILY

It's up, up... and
Local house takes to the sky

DAN THOMAS
Record Staff Writer

Yesterday started like any other in midtown America. But locals were about to witness a unique event.

At 8.15 a.m., two nurses from the Shady Oaks Retirement Village, A.J. and George, arrived to take Carl Fredricksen to his new residence in the Village following his conviction for assault on a construction worker.

"I've never seen anything like it in my entire life!"

A.J. says: "We knocked on the door to tell Mr. Fredricksen that we were here. He said he needed to say one last goodbye to the place. We thought he was going to the bathroom for the eightieth time!"

Heads up! *Astonished window-shoppers gape as the house soars overhead.*

Photo: Matt Walker

Photo: Victoria Taylor

Where's the party? *A tiny tot watches as balloons fly past her bedroom window.*

According to A.J.'s coworker, George, after a few minutes an enormous dark shadow came over them and they looked up and saw a large tarp sliding off the roof with thousands of balloons under it. "There was a

RECORD

away!

First on the scene *George and A.J. from the Shady Oaks Retirement Village were the first to see the house lift off.*

loud noise as the house ripped away from its foundations and then it took off down the street. I've never seen anything like it in my entire life!" says George.

Mr. Robinson, a diner at a nearby sushi restaurant, says at first he thought the flying house might be "a novelty air balloon."

Experts confirm that the unusual transportation would have taken a lot of planning and have called Mr. Fredricksen "determined."

Later, witness reports also claimed that a young Wilderness Explorer may have been "on board" when the house took flight, but these reports are yet to be confirmed.

Calculated *Experts say the number of balloons needed to lift the house had to be carefully worked out.*

19

CHARLES F. MUNTZ

With charm and cunning that made him one of the first celebrity explorers, Charles F. Muntz enjoyed hobnobbing among the world's political elite and was the handsome and clever rebel of Tinseltown during its heyday.

Muntz attracted legions of adoring fans, but the most loyal were those with the thirst for adventure. The larger-than-life explorer sought freedom in the wild, where dreams awaited discovery. He traveled the globe to unearth priceless treasures, from ancient artifacts to fossils of extinct and unknown fauna.

Charles Muntz was Ellie's hero. She wanted to be a famous explorer just like him when she grew up.

This postage stamp shows a dirigible just like the one Charles Muntz flies.

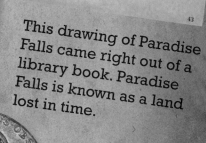

"Paradise Falls, a land lost in time"

43

This drawing of Paradise Falls came right out of a library book. Paradise Falls is known as a land lost in time.

Ellie really wanted to go to Paradise Falls in South America.

Ellie loved unusual coins. This one has a rare species of bird on it. It looks like a toucan.

A real explorer tries to find all sorts of animals. Ellie wanted to see lots of creatures on her travels.

Ellie found this flower in the front of her clubhouse.

ELLIE'S ADVENTURE BOOK

Shhh! You must promise not to tell anyone about Ellie's Adventure Book. It's top secret! It shows all the adventures Ellie wanted to go on and all the stuff she was going to see. Take a look but make sure no one else is around!

This feather came from a pigeon that Ellie admired.

Pan American Parrot

SOUTH AMERICA

Magellans

DRAKES

ANTARTICA

These parrots have got very bright feathers. Wouldn't it be great to see a real parrot in the jungle?

Every explorer needs a map. Ellie drew one of South America so she would know exactly where to go.

Ellie wanted to move her clubhouse to Paradise Falls. What a view that would be!

Charles Muntz is looking for a big bird. Ellie drew a picture of what she thought the bird looked like.

Ellie loved learning about animals, especially unusual ones like this platypus.

MY ADVENTURE BOOK

Ellie's Adventure Book had lots of blank pages for all the adventures she would have.

21

CHARLES F. MUNTZ

In the 1930s, explorer Charles F. Muntz had it all—film-star looks, friends in high places, lots of charisma. Fans went crazy for news of Muntz's latest exploits in his dirigible, the *Spirit of Adventure*. Then it all ended. Accused of faking the skeleton of a giant bird he found at Paradise Falls, Muntz was kicked out of the National Explorer's Society, and his career took a nosedive.

Muntz returned to Paradise Falls hoping to capture another giant bird—this time alive! Sadly, none of his traps have worked.

Home From Home

On the mountain, Muntz sets up home in his airship placed in a huge cave. He lives here with his pack of dogs, who are always on the lookout for any unwanted guests.

Long Wait

Muntz promised the world that he would not come back until he had captured the "Monster of Paradise Falls." Now an old man, he is still waiting...

Muntz was the poster boy for an entire generation of explorers and adventurers.

"Adventure is out there!"

Muntz still fits into the brown leather flight jacket he wore as a young man!

Fit as a fiddle, Muntz doesn't really need a cane. However, it can come in handy as a weapon!

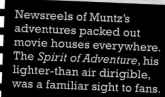

Newsreels of Muntz's adventures packed out movie houses everywhere. The *Spirit of Adventure*, his lighter-than air dirigible, was a familiar sight to fans.

No part of the globe was off limits to Muntz, and his trips always made the news. But it was his visit to Paradise Falls that hit the headlines like no other.

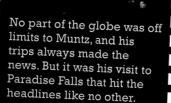

Press and fans alike were there to greet Muntz as he returned from the expedition. A natural showman, Muntz soaked up the applause.

The world watched, shocked, as the National Explorer's Society stripped Muntz of his membership. Muntz was determined to get his good name back—and his fans.

Suspicious Mind

After years with only his faithful dogs for company, Muntz has become wary of strangers. What if they have come to capture the precious bird?

RUSSELL

Russell is a Junior Wilderness Explorer who is eager for adventure! A member of Tribe 54, Sweat Lodge 12, Russell only needs his Assisting the Elderly badge to become a Senior Wilderness Explorer. Little does he know that his quest will send him on a BIG adventure!

Russell is determined to assist Mr. Fredricksen. Russell loves learning new skills and works hard for his badges. Once Russell learns something, he rarely forgets it.

Did you know?

• Russell's only experience with camping is visiting the downtown Camping Museum!

Russell wears his colorful sash of badges with pride.

Call Of Duty

Russell takes his Wilderness Explorer tasks very seriously. He enjoys helping animals and is "a friend to all," even giant birds and strange dogs.

Russell is always on-the-go, whether it's practicing karate or flying kites.

Russell has found the perfect spot for his new badge, next to his Extreme Mountaineering and Swimming badges.

Talkative Russell is at a loss for words when he finds himself stuck on the porch of Mr. Fredricksen's floating house. There was nothing in the Wilderness Explorer Manual about flying houses!

"The wilderness must be explored!"

Sky High

Until now, Russell had only flown toy planes in his bedroom. He can't quite believe he's piloting a floating house—and neither can Carl!

Heart To Heart

Russell confides in Carl and tells him that he doesn't see his dad very often. He is sure his dad will come to his Explorer ceremony though. Then maybe he could show Russell how to build a tent.

WILDERNESS EXPLORER

I blow this horn to call the Explorers to action. tI need a lot of puff to get my horn to make noise!

My Wilderness Explorer hat is great if I haven't had time to comb my hair.

The Wilderness Explorer's motto is: "An Explorer is a friend to all, be it plants or fish or tiny mole." Some people say it doesn't rhyme but I like it! Wilderness Explorers are always ready for action. We have a smart uniform and a backpack filled with everything we need in case we find ourselves stuck in the wild... though we usually don't go further than our Explorer's Hut. Here's a guide to all the things that an Explorer needs! Caw-car, rarr!

I'm sure my weather badge will come in handy some day soon.

Sometimes I get a bit tangled up putting my toggle on!

My Sash

My Wilderness Explorer's sash is my favorite part of our uniform. I have tons of badges. When I finished stitching all of my badges on my sash, I earned my Sewing badge!

My Gadgets

Every Explorer needs special gadgets. My GPS tells me exactly where I am anywhere in the world!

Wilderness Call

1. First put your fingers and thumbs into a "W" shape.

2. Then make a flying bird shape with your hands. Don't forget to make a "Caw-car" noise!

3. Now growl like a big bear with sharp claws—rarr! You've just done your first Wilderness Call!

My Backpack

I always strap lots of stuff to my backpack, like my water bottle, cup, and self-heating canteen. Exploring makes you thirsty!

BADGES

The best thing about being a Wilderness Explorer is earning merit badges. Here are just some of the badges that you can get and what you have to do to earn them.

I can tie knots really well, so I earned my Knot Tying badge! It's untying knots that's tricky.

For my Theater Badge, I had to pretend to be a tree. That sure was a lot of standing still.

My Boating Badge was a tough one. I think I prefer being on dry land instead of water!

When I got my Bird Spotting Badge, I was the only one to spot the Lesser Spotted Woodpecker.

I painted a picture of a little doggie for my Art Badge. Dogs are the best!

The Assisting the Elderly Badge is the only one I still need. Then I'll be a Senior Wilderness Explorer!

I learned all about leaves and flowers for my Botany Badge.

LET'S EXPLORE!

Like other areas of life, the world of exploring attracts all types of people with all types of dreams. Here are four explorers who have been on their own unique journeys.

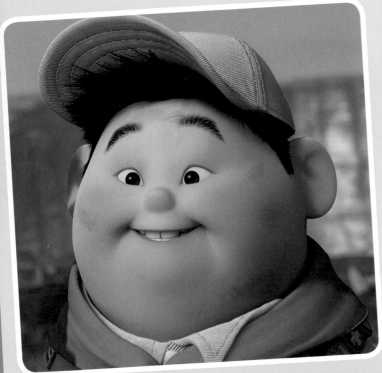

RUSSELL

Style: Eager
Experience: Hasn't traveled very far
Top Moment: Flying in a house!
Companion: Mr. Fredricksen

Russell doesn't have much in the way of adventurous experience, but he makes up for it with boundless enthusiasm. He's in awe of older and wiser explorers and tries to learn from them, but when he's in a bind it's often Russell's initiative that gets him out of trouble.

YOUNG ELLIE

Style: Go-getter
Experience: Mainly in her imaginatio
Top Moment: Playing in her clubhouse
Companion: Young Carl

Bold and feisty Ellie never gets to do most of the things she has listed in her Adventure Book, but that doesn't get her down one bit. Ellie knows that with the right attitude, everyday life can be one big adventure.

CARL FREDRICKSEN

Style: Reluctant

Experience: Watching news footage of Charles F. Muntz

Top Moment: Seeing the Shady Oaks nurses' faces as his house took off

Companion: Russell or Ellie

Carl is a whiz at practical things like working out the number of balloons to control a flying house. Carl finds it hard to work with others, but discovers he's not too old to change his ways.

CHARLES F. MUNTZ

Style: Flashy

Experience: Traveled the world

Top Moment: Becoming a member of the National Explorer's Society

Exploring Companion: Faithful pack of dogs

For Charles F. Muntz, it's all about the glory. Fame and prestige mean as much to him as his discoveries, if not more. This makes him a risk-taker and quite an ego-maniac.

STORMY WEATHER

Carl's house is not long into its maiden voyage when Russell spots a group of cumulonimbus clouds in the distance. A storm is brewing! He just knew that his Weather badge would come in handy one day. The trip to Paradise Falls doesn't look like it's going to be smooth sailing!

Peace And Quiet

Carl picked the wrong time to get some quiet. When Russell's chattering gets on his nerves, Carl switches off his hearing aid. The trouble is Russell is trying to tell Carl about the fast-approaching storm!

As the storm knocks the house from side to side, Russell manages to rescue his backpack. However, he almost manages to fall out of the house himself!

Carl's house is heading toward the eye of the storm.

Lightning-quick

Russell may understand how cumulonimbus clouds form to make lightning but can he work out how to get the house out of the storm's path?

The lightning makes Carl realize that something could go badly wrong.

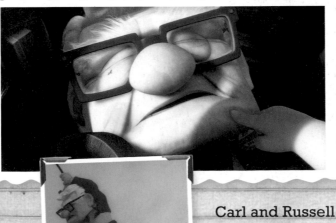

Afternoon Nap

The moving house knocks Carl unconscious. When he awakes, Russell has steered them to safety using his Explorer skills.

Carl and Russell land the house near Paradise Falls! They may be happy to stay here but the house has other ideas and the pair must find a way to keep the house from floating away from them!

Crest feathers add an extra inch to Kevin's height.

Large beak is great for eating things like balloons and walking canes!

Brightly colored feathers make it difficult for Kevin to hide.

What A Fowl-up!

Carl tries to distract Russell by telling him to find a snipe who is eating his azaleas. To Carl's shock, Russell finds one—in the jungles of South America! Russell names this nervous bird Kevin but later finds out that *he* is actually a *she*!

Clawed feet help Kevin scale rocks.

KEVIN

Jungles are full of lush green plants and unusual flowers but the last thing you would expect to see is a 12-foot-tall bird! Unless, of course, you're Charles F. Muntz, who has made it his life's work to find this flightless, feathered creature with the help of his vicious pack of dogs.

When Kevin first appears, Russell thinks he has found the snipe, until Carl explains that there is no such thing.

Flying High

Kevin is one mischievous bird. Just like a weather vane, she perches on top of Carl's house and helps herself to one of his balloons. After all, Carl's got a lot to spare!

Birds Of A Feather

In the start of their journey, Russell and Carl have a love—hate relationship with Kevin: Russell loves the bird while Carl hates the "feathered freak!"

Most birds eat a healthy diet of plants, seeds, and berries. Kevin prefers chocolate that Russell feeds him!

Did you know?

- Kevin is the proud mother of several baby birds.
- Kevin's home is in a group of twisty rocks called a labyrinth.

DUG

Dug is a typical dog—almost. He's full of energy, incredibly loving, and can TALK! Yes—this dog talks! His master, Charles F. Muntz, made collars for his pack of dogs that translate their thoughts into human language. And Dug certainly has a lot of thoughts. Dug isn't all talk, though, and one day he's sure he'll get to show how reliable he really is.

Keeping Track

Dug isn't the brightest pooch. When the red light on his collar flashes, it means Muntz's pack knows where he is. Dug just thinks it looks pretty.

Carl and Russell are more than a little shocked to meet a talking dog, especially when one of the first things Dug says to them is "I can smell you!"

When a dog wags his tail, it means he is happy. Dug is always wagging his tail.

The only time Dug concentrates is when he thinks he sees a squirrel. SQUIRREL!!!

"I've just met you and I love you."

Man's Best Friend

Dug's a bit confused. He knows that Muntz is his master and that he is part of Alpha's pack but he really and truly loves Carl and Russell. He wishes Carl could be his master.

Dug's large nose helps him track animals of all shapes and sizes... SQUIRREL!!!

Four-legged Friend

Dug has been sent on a special mission by Muntz's chief dog, Alpha, to find a giant bird. Dug is sure that when he does locate it, Muntz's pack will like him. All Dug wants is for others to be his friend.

These buttons let Dug speak in many languages, like Spanish or Japanese.

Did you know?

• When Dug loses Kevin, Alpha makes him wear the Cone of Shame around his neck. It really does make Dug feel ashamed.

THE JOURNEY

Carl wanted to land the house right next to Paradise Falls, but his plans were derailed when the storm brought the house down to earth too soon. He and Russell are forced to make the last part of the journey on foot, hauling the floating house above them. And that's when the adventure really takes off...

Night falls, and they set up camp. Russell can't get the tent up, but the bonfire manages to keep them warm.

In rocky terrain, the trio are joined by Dug, a dog sent by Muntz to track the giant bird.

Carl and Russell descend into the jungle, where Russell's chocolate attracts the interest of a giant bird.

The house lands on the edge of a tall tepui. Paradise Falls is only ten miles away, but there's a large chasm to cross.

As the wind whips the house aloft again, Carl hangs on by a garden hose. Carl and Russell will have to tow it the rest of the way!

6 The next morning the group is rudely interrupted by more of Muntz's dogs: Alpha, Beta, and Gamma.

7 The dogs take them through a desolate area to a cave. Here, they are met by Muntz himself.

8 After escaping from Muntz, they try to help Kevin return to her nest in the rocky labyrinth.

9 Carl blames Russell and Dug for involving him in an adventure he didn't want. He sets off for Paradise Falls alone with the house.

10 At Paradise Falls, Carl thinks he's at the end of his journey. But a message from Ellie changes his mind.

High In The Sky

When traveling to the towering falls, it is best to use an airplane or dirigible. Alternatively, a flying house will do but these are harder to come by.

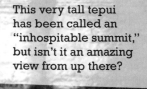

This very tall tepui has been called an "inhospitable summit," but isn't it an amazing view from up there?

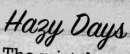

Hazy Days

The mist that often hangs over the rocky terrain can play tricks on people's eyes, making the strangely shaped rocks look like people or even dogs.

Thick Jungle

Just when you think you're lost in the jungle, you'll stumble upon a clearing—perfect for setting up camp.

A huge waterfall decends from the tepui.

PARADISE FALLS

The stunning Paradise Falls lies deep in South America, surrounded by lush jungles and rocky terrain filled with luscious plants and animals. Many explorers, such as botanists and surveyors, have visited this "land lost in time" in hopes of making a marvelous discovery. Others have traveled here simply for the amazing views. Mysteriously, few have returned to tell the tale.

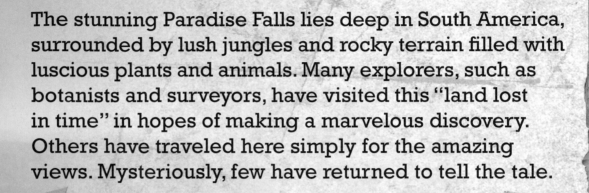

Clear Skies

The weather is usually clear around the tepui (also known as a tabletop mountain). But sometimes patchy fog creeps in...

In The Undergrowth

The jungle bushes and grasses are great camouflage for tall birds. Birds better watch out for hidden traps, though!

ALPHA

Alpha is always focused on the task at hand, and expects the same from the rest of his pack.

Alpha is the leader of Charles F. Muntz's pack of dogs. This sinister Doberman takes his duties seriously, rewarding his dogs when they obey but scolding them when they don't. Under Muntz's orders, he sends Dug, Beta, and Gamma out on the hunt for a giant bird. For Alpha, failure-to-find is not an option.

Cone Of Shame

Alpha begins to regret his plan to send Dug off on his own to find the bird when he returns alone. Disappointed, Alpha puts Dug in the Cone of Shame, the ultimate collared-canine humiliation.

Alpha sometimes has to get Muntz to fix his collar when the translator malfunctions.

Adaptable Alpha

Alpha's alert ears and brilliant eyesight make him an excellent tracker. However, he can turn his paw at just about anything his master requires, even when it comes to serving dinner.

Canine Orders

Alpha's henchdogs respect their leader—until his collar breaks and his voice sounds funny. Barking orders in a high-pitched voice just isn't as intimidating!

Alpha keeps track of his pack by using the video technology on the dogs' collars.

"Mayhaps you desire to challenge the ranking that I have been assigned by my strength and cunning?"

Tricks Of The Trade

Alpha has three tricks that are guaranteed to frighten:
1. Hang around with other scary-looking dogs.
2. Always keep your fangs visible.
3. Growl loudly!

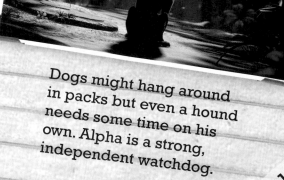

Did you know?

• Alpha often uses ten words when three would do: "Do you not agree with that which I am saying to you?" aka "Don't you agree?"!

Dogs might hang around in packs but even a hound needs some time on his own. Alpha is a strong, independent watchdog.

BETA & GAMMA

Beta and Gamma are considered the brains and brawn of Charles F. Muntz's dog pack. This mismatched pair have been trained by their master to obey his every wish, including trying to find the giant bird. Led by Alpha, they look up to their leader but firmly look down on Dug!

The dogs' collars feature lights that let them see into caves and stop them from getting scared in dark places.

Canine Collars

Beta and Gamma have talking collars like their fellow pack members. However, even they are at a loss for words when they lose track of the giant bird.

" I'm getting prunes and denture cream ! "

Beta

Beta is one tough Rottweiler. He is Alpha's lieutenant and the leader has a lot of respect for him. Alpha has even been known to call Beta "wise"—a rare compliment!

Beta and Gamma have both picked up on one of Alpha's top tips: if you bare your teeth at someone, they'll begin to see things your way.

Gamma's sharp hearing helps him hunt down any creature.

Bow Down

While Alpha, Beta, and Gamma are all part of the same pack, it is Alpha who is clearly in charge. He's the only one that can make this doggy duo tremble with fear.

Flying Dogs

Beta and Gamma fly Muntz's fighter planes! Beta's flying name is Grey Leader while Gamma answers to Grey 2.

Gamma

Gamma is a bulldog and Alpha's third-in-command. He wants to be like his leader but is easily distracted, especially if he sees a tennis ball that needs chasing.

THE CHASE IS ON!

Russell is upset that Carl has abandoned Kevin and decides to go and help his feathered friend alone. Using a leaf blower to hoist him into the air, he takes to the sky and heads toward the *Spirit of Adventure*. But everything gets a bit out of hand and Russell realizes he may need help after all!

Going Overboard

In order to reach Russell on the dirigible, Carl has to get the house airborne, but there's only one way to make it light enough to rise. Everything inside must go!

Air Wars

As Russell tries to dodge the dogs, two more battles are taking place on the dirigible: Carl is now aboard and fencing with Muntz, while Dug tussles with Alpha.

Hanging On

The garden hose is slippery and Russell can't climb up it and get back into the house. He ends up sliding across the window of the dirigible on his belly instead!

Bow Wow Ouch!

It only takes a cry of "Squirrel!!" from Russell to throw the pilot pooches into confusion.

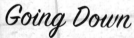

Ready...Take Aim...

With the dogs defeated, Carl, Kevin, and Dug manage to join Russell in the house, but the danger isn't over. Muntz has a rifle!

Going Down

Muntz's bullet takes out half the balloons and the house crashes onto the dirigible. The friends leap to safety but Muntz is not so lucky. He and the house plummet together.

New Adventures

Carl finally loses Muntz for good, but he loses his house too. Somehow it doesn't matter any more. He has begun a new adventure—the adventure of making life-long friends.

ADVENTURE IS ALL AROUND US!

Adventures don't just happen in faraway places! Carl believed that the big adventure of his life with Ellie would be their trip to Paradise Falls. It has taken him years to realize what Ellie had always understood: sometimes the everyday stuff is the biggest adventure of all!

Thanks for the adventure— now go have a new one!

Love, Ellie

. In Ellie's last message to Carl, she gave him her blessing to live life to the fullest without her.

Double Dream

Carl thought that Ellie's greatest dreams were to travel far and wide. But Ellie's Adventure Book was actually filled with pictures of the two of them sharing simple moments together.

Happy House

Newlyweds Carl and Ellie set up home in Ellie's old clubhouse. The couple worked hard to turn the house from a dump into a dream home full of happy memories.

Sad Parting

The Fredricksens expected they would grow old together. It was a shock when Carl one day found himself all alone.

Moving On

In South America, Carl reaches a turning point when he holds Ellie's message in one hand and Russell's sash of badges in the other. Will he look to the past—or to the future?

Ellie created the shrine's centerpiece— a magnificent painting of Paradise Falls.

Best Of Friends

Going on an adventure in a flying house can be lots of fun but Carl and Russell realize that sometimes it's the boring things you remember most, like eating ice cream and counting cars with a friend.

LONDON, NEW YORK,
MELBOURNE, MUNICH, AND DELHI

Senior Designer Lynne Moulding
Senior Editor Laura Gilbert
Editor Julia March
Managing Editor Catherine Saunders
Art Director Lisa Lanzarini
Publishing Manager Simon Beecroft
Category Publisher Alex Allan
Production Editor Clare McLean
Print Production Nick Seston

First published in the United States in 2009
by DK Publishing
375 Hudson Street
New York, New York 10014

09 10 11 12 13 10 9 8 7 6 5 4 3 2 1
UD167 – 04/09

DK books are available at special
discounts when purchased in bulk for
sales promotions, premiums, fundraising,
or educational use. For details, contact:
DK Publishing Special Markets,
375 Hudson Street,
New York, New York 10014
SpecialSales@dk.com

A catalog record for this book is
available from the Library of Congress.

ISBN: 978-0-7566-4589-2

Color reproduction by Alta Image, UK
Printed and bound in the USA by Lake Books

**Discover more at
www.dk.com**

DK would like to thank:
Leeann Alameda, Kelly Bonbright, Kathleen
Chanover, Ed Chen, Ronnie del Carmen,
Pete Docter, Magen Farrar, Cherie
Hammond, Stella Koh, Erik Langley, Holly
Lloyd, LeighAnna MacFadden, Desiree
Mourad, Ricky Nierva, Silvia Palara, Burt
Peng, Jonas Rivera, Kiki Thorpe, Jesse
Weglein, Clay Welch, Chris Wells, and
Timothy Zohr at Pixar Animation Studios
and Graham Barnard, Lauren Kressel, and
Laura Uyeda at Disney Publishing.

48